the CRiTTER club

Amy and the Missing Puppy

by Callie Barkley ♥ illustrated by Marsha Riti

SCHOLASTIC INC.

ISBN 978-0-545-56759-6

12 11 10 9 8 7 6 5 4   15 16 17 18/0

Printed in the U.S.A.   40

First Scholastic printing, May 2013

Designed by Laura Roode

Table of Contents

chapter 1

Spring Break Blues

Amy felt herself starting to blush. Her cheeks felt warm, then hot. Amy shook her short, light brown hair over her freckled face. She hoped it would hide her bright pink cheeks. *At least I'm not at school,* Amy thought. *I hate blushing in front of the whole class!*

In fact Amy wouldn't be back at

her school, Santa Vista Elementary, for one whole week. It was the Friday night before spring break. Amy was in her bedroom with her best friends, Marion, Ellie, and Liz. They had a sleepover almost every Friday. This week, it was Amy's turn to host.

The girls were finishing up a game of MASH. Amy held up the paper that had made her blush. She pointed to the name of her future husband.

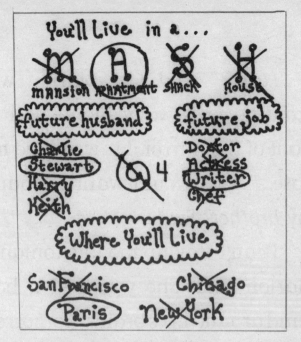

Liz, Marion, and Ellie squealed.

"You're so lucky, Amy!" Ellie said, shaking her hands to dry her newly painted nails. Stewart was Liz's big brother. He was twelve. All the girls, except for Liz, thought he was the cutest.

"Lucky?" said Liz. Marion was braiding Liz's wavy blond hair in front of the mirror. Liz wrinkled her nose. "Who would want to marry my *brother*? Ew."

"I can't stay up too late tonight," Marion said. She wrapped a hair band around Liz's braid. "Tomorrow my mom and I are taking Coco to a big horse show!"

Coco was Marion's brown pure-bred horse. Marion was a great rider. Together, Marion and Coco had won tons of blue ribbons! "We'll be out of town for most of the week," Marion added, her green eyes twinkling.

"Me too," said Liz. Liz and her family were going to the beach. "I can't wait! A whole week of sun,

sand, and best of all, no home-work!" Liz flopped back onto Amy's bed. "I'm going to bring my easel and paint box. I'll paint you each a sunset!" Amy loved Liz's paintings. She was such a good artist!

Ellie sighed and fluffed her red pil-low. "Well, I'll be here in Santa Vista *all week,*" she said, plopping down. Her tight black curls bounced over her headband. Ellie tossed her head dramatically. "BOR-ing! But at least my Nana Gloria is coming to stay!"

Ellie's grandmother was moving in with her family. "She's bringing over some boxes—and her parrot, Lenny! I want to teach him a song. Then we can sing a duet!"

Ellie grabbed a pink hairbrush. She flicked on Amy's MP3 player. Singing along with a pop song, Ellie belted into her hairbrush microphone. Ellie always sang loudly and with feeling, like an actress on a stage.

"How about you, Amy?" Ellie said. "What are you going to do this week?"

Amy's heart sank a little. Her friends all had somewhere to go or something to do. She didn't.

Amy's parents were divorced and Amy lived with her mom

in Santa Vista. Her dad lived in Orange Blossom, the next town over. Amy sighed as she remembered that she couldn't even go visit Dad this break because he was away on business.

Amy shrugged. "Read?" she said. "I do have a brand-new Nancy Drew book. Count the change in my piggy bank? Dust my sticker collection?" Her friends giggled, but Amy was only half joking. What *was* she going to do?

"I guess I'll help my mom at

the clinic," Amy said. Amy's mom, Dr. Melanie Purvis, was a veterinarian. She ran a vet clinic in the house next door. Pets from all over Santa Vista came for their checkups. Other times, animals came when they were sick or hurt. Amy loved animals of all kinds. She also loved spending time at her mom's clinic.

As if reading her mind, Amy's cat Milly crawled out from under the bed. She climbed into Amy's lap. "Milly will keep me company. Right, Milly?"

Only seven days until next Friday—their next sleepover. Then they would all be together again.

Oh, well, thought Amy. *Spring break can't last forever.*

chapter 2

A New Friend

Monday morning was slow at the vet clinic. Amy sat behind the front desk. Her mom was busy in back, checking on a sick hamster. Gail, the vet assistant, had gone out for coffee. It looked like Amy was in charge. Normally, being in charge made Amy feel important, but not today. Instead, she wondered what her friends were up to. She sighed. *Nothing ever happens in Santa Vista*, she thought.

Amy looked down at the day's list of appointments.

The next patient wouldn't be there for another fifteen minutes.

APPOINTMENTS

MONDAY

8 Tracy (cocker spaniel): teeth cleaning

9 Cooper (orange tabby): vaccination

10 Rufus (Saint Bernard Puppy): 6 month checkup

11 Lulu (Goldfish): ich treatment

12

Amy had already watered the flower beds out front, and filled all the treat jars in the waiting room with Fitter Critter healthy pet snacks. Amy tucked the half-empty bag of treats into the pocket of her yellow hoodie.

Since she had some time to spare, she decided to read her book. She put on her purple reading glasses and opened her new Nancy Drew mystery.

Nancy started by making a list of suspects. "Who *could* have taken the prize-winning pony from Alice's barn during the night?" she asked herself.

The next-door neighbor, old Mr. Gilbert, came to mind. He sure had been gruff when Nancy met him. Plus, Alice had said that in the whole ten years since she'd moved in, Mr. Gilbert had never once smiled or waved over the fence. Sometimes she felt like Mr. Gilbert didn't want a neighbor at all.

Amy heard a car pull up outside. As she looked out the window, the door of a fancy silver car opened. Amy squinted as a figure stepped out of the car.

Amy gasped. It was none other than *Marge Sullivan*!

Marge Sullivan had lived in Santa Vista for a few years. She lived alone, way out on the edge of town. Her house was huge—like a mansion.

Amy didn't know anyone who had ever been inside it. People said Ms. Sullivan was a billionaire. She hardly ever came into town. When she did, she didn't talk much. Kids and even some parents were afraid of her. Now and then, some brave kids would ring her doorbell on Halloween, but they always ran away before she came to the door.

Amy smoothed her hair and sat up very straight in her chair as

Ms. Sullivan strode in. Ms. Sullivan didn't seem like the kind of person you should slouch around.

The older woman looked down at Amy. It felt like a cold *who-are-you?* look. Amy opened her mouth to speak. But nothing came out! Amy felt the warmth rising in her cheeks. Oh no! She was starting to blush.

All of a sudden, Amy heard the jangle of a dog collar. Around the desk came a blur of brown and white fur. Amy felt a paw on either shoulder as she toppled off her chair. The next thing she knew, she

was on the floor and a drooly Saint Bernard puppy was covering her face with doggy kisses.

Amy giggled and squealed. The Fitter Critter treats fell out of her pocket and scattered on to the floor. The puppy sniffed them before he gulped down three.

"Bad boy, Rufus! Naughty!" Ms. Sullivan said sternly. The puppy returned to Ms. Sullivan's side. He sat and looked up at her. His tail was wagging a mile a minute.

Still giggling, Amy picked herself up off the floor. She dried her face with the sleeve of her hoodie.

"Well, it looks like you've made a new friend," Ms. Sullivan said to Amy.

Amy looked up. For a split second, she thought she saw Ms. Sullivan's mouth turn up at the corners. Was that a *smile*? Amy had never seen Ms. Sullivan smile before. She'd never seen her with a puppy before, either. *Huh*, she thought. *Ms. Sullivan doesn't seem like a pet person.*

Just then Dr. Purvis, Amy's mother, came into the waiting room. "Hello, Marge! Hello, Rufus!" she said. She led them to an exam room.

Amy looked down at her favorite yellow hoodie. Below each shoulder was one perfect muddy paw print. *Guess Rufus found the wet flower bed on his way in!* Amy thought. She laughed and tried to wipe off the prints with a paper towel. It didn't help.

Rufus had left his mark.

chapter 3

Taking Out the Trash

That night, after dinner, Amy was curled up on the sofa. Her nose was buried deep in the pages of her mystery.

Nancy followed the small hoofprints across the muddy patch of grass. She could just make them out by the light of the bright, full moon.

Suddenly, Nancy heard a rustling coming from the trees!

She froze. Lifting her flashlight, she aimed the beam into the woods. There it was again! The rustling grew louder and louder, until . . .

Branches parted and the flashlight beam lit up a face— the face of a man. Nancy gasped. It was Mr. Gilbert!

"Amy!" Amy's mom called from the kitchen. "Please come take out the trash!"

Amy sighed and put her book down. "Coming!" she called. She hurried into the kitchen. The faster she took out the trash, the sooner she could get back to her book! She grabbed the full trash bag and dashed out the back door.

Amy didn't bother to turn on the backyard light. She lifted the metal trash can lid and dumped the bag inside. Amy dropped the lid, letting it crash down with a loud *bang*.

Then, she heard it. Amy *thought* she heard a rustling sound! She could have sworn it came from the shrubs between her backyard and the clinic next door. Amy peered into the dark, shadowy shrubs, but couldn't see anything. She stood still, listening. Nothing.

Then the wind picked up. Shrubs and tree branches waved. Leaves rustled. Amy thought the air smelled like rain.

Amy relaxed. Her book was putting ideas into her head!

Back inside, Amy found her mom on the sofa with a big bowl of popcorn. "Want to watch that new spy movie?" Dr. Purvis asked.

Amy smiled. No school tomorrow meant no bedtime. Amy flopped down on the sofa. She could read her book later. Movie night with her mom was the best.

Outside, the first few raindrops tapped against the windows.

A Surprise Guest

Halfway through the movie, the doorbell rang. Dr. Purvis pressed pause on the remote control. "Who could that be?" she said. "It's kind of late . . ."

Amy followed her to the front door. She stood next to her mom as she opened it.

Just then a streak of lightning lit

up the dark sky. Thunder clapped. Amy jumped. She grabbed the back of her mom's sweater.

Marge Sullivan was standing on the front porch.

Water dripped from her rain hat. Her black raincoat was soaked. Her cheeks even looked wet. Amy realized it wasn't from the rain. Ms. Sullivan was crying.

"I'm really sorry to bother you," Ms. Sullivan said to Dr. Purvis. "It's Rufus. He's . . . gone!"

Amy's mom invited her in. Amy's heart was still pounding in

her chest, but she followed as her mom led the way to the kitchen. Dr. Purvis took Ms. Sullivan's wet things. Ms. Sullivan had a seat at the table.

"I'll make you some tea," said Dr. Purvis as she put the kettle on. "You tell us what happened."

Amy stood in the doorway and listened.

"I let Rufus out after dinner," Ms. Sullivan began. "The backyard is fenced in.

"When it got windy, I called him in," Ms. Sullivan went on, "but Rufus didn't come. When I went out to look for him, I found a hole by the fence. He must have dug it out."

Ms. Sullivan's lower lip shook. "My poor Rufus. He's out in this storm, all alone."

Dr. Purvis put a hand on Ms. Sullivan's shoulder. "He can't have gotten far," she said. "Let me make some phone calls." She took her cell phone and left the room.

Amy didn't know what to say or do. Ms. Sullivan had always seemed stern and serious. Now, here she was crying in Amy's kitchen. When the kettle whistled, Amy made her a cup of tea. She set it on the table with the milk and sugar.

"Thank you, Amy," Ms. Sullivan said softly. Amy was surprised Ms. Sullivan knew her name.

Dr. Purvis came back in. "Well, I called the police. I also called the animal shelter over in Orange Blossom. If they hear anything or spot Rufus, they'll let us know right away." Dr. Purvis sighed. "It's really a shame Santa Vista doesn't have its own animal shelter."

Dr. Purvis and Ms. Sullivan talked a while longer. Amy went upstairs. As she got ready for bed, she could hear her mother and Ms. Sullivan in the front hall. "I'll help you look in the morning, Marge," her mom was saying. "He'll be easier to spot in the daylight."

Amy heard the front door close. As she opened her book, she wondered how Nancy Drew would solve this mystery.

Clues . . ., thought Amy. *Rufus must have left some clues behind.* If Amy could find them, maybe *she* could help find Rufus. It would be Amy's first case.

chapter 5

The First Clue!

By Tuesday morning the storm had passed. The sun was warm as Amy walked next door. She'd help out at the clinic for the morning. Then, she'd call Ellie. She missed her friends so much!

How many times have I walked down this sidewalk? Amy wondered. *A million times?* That's how she knew there were fifteen sidewalk squares between the two houses. She counted them in her head as she walked.

But this morning, on square number nine, Amy stopped in her tracks.

Right there on the sidewalk were several paw prints. Amy felt like she had seen one exactly like it yesterday. Amy remembered the paw prints on her favorite yellow hoodie!

Rufus had been here *since the rainstorm*! Otherwise, the rain would have washed the prints away.

Amy smiled. This was a clue! But now what? What would Nancy Drew do? And then she knew.

Amy hurried back into her house. She returned with a small green notebook and her favorite blue pen. She opened the notebook and began to write.

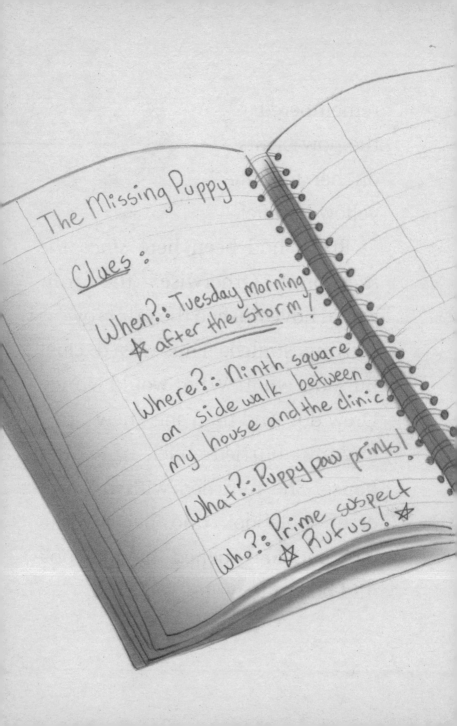

It was a start! Amy was on her way to solving the mystery of the missing puppy!

chapter 6

Rufus Was Here

Amy was in charge at the front
desk all morning while her mom
and Ms. Sullivan were out looking
for Rufus. Gail, the vet assistant,
was busy giving some checkups
while Amy watered the flower bed
out front and refilled the treat jars.

Dr. Purvis finally returned
around lunchtime.

"Any luck?" Amy asked her.

Her mom shook her head no. "We drove all over. No sign of him."

Amy pulled out her notebook. "I found one sign of him," she said. She explained how the print on the sidewalk matched the Rufus prints on her hoodie.

Amy's mom smiled. "Great detective work!" she said. "The more people looking, the better chance we have of finding Rufus."

Amy walked home and had lunch. After she finished her sandwich, she called Ellie's house.

"Amy!" Ellie cried when she came to the phone. "Am I glad to hear from you!" There was really loud squawking in the background. "Nana Gloria's parrot is driving me nuts!"

Amy couldn't make out Lenny the parrot's words. But it sounded like he was singing a song. Well, if you could call all that squawking *singing*.

Amy told Ellie about Rufus going missing. She also told Ellie about the paw print. "Do you want to come over?" Amy asked. "We could look for more clues together."

The words were barely out of Amy's mouth. Ellie shouted, "I'll be right over!" and hung up.

Ellie lived only three streets over. A few minutes later, she rode up on her bike. Amy went outside to meet her.

"Oh, Amy," Ellie said, giving her a hug. She was out of breath. "I love Lenny, but that bird does not stop talking *or* singing!"

Amy held back a giggle. She knew Ellie didn't think it was funny.

Amy told Ellie all about the case: how Rufus got loose, when he went missing, and what he looked like. She showed Ellie the paw prints on

the sidewalk. Together, they looked around for more.

"Here!" Ellie said, pointing at the sidewalk. They were past the clinic. A trail of paw prints led further down the sidewalk.

"Yes! Rufus prints, for sure!" Amy cried. She pulled out her notebook and jotted down these clues.

The girls slowly followed the trail. "I don't blame Rufus for running away from mean old Ms. Sullivan," said Ellie. "I would run away too!"

They were in front of the house on the other side of the clinic. The paw prints were disappearing.

"I don't know," Amy replied. She thought about how sad Ms. Sullivan was about losing Rufus. It was clear she really loved him. "Maybe Ms. Sullivan isn't as bad as everyone thinks. You know what they say about judging a book by its cover."

Ellie stopped walking. She looked at Amy. She rolled her eyes. "You *would* talk about books at a time like this, Amy."

The girls looked down. Suddenly

there were no more paw prints.
They were at a dead end.

"Now what?" Ellie said.

Amy looked down at her notebook. She turned to a blank page.

"If we were Rufus, where would
we go?" asked Amy.

They thought about it as they
walked back to Amy's house. They

decided they would spend the rest
of the afternoon making a new list.

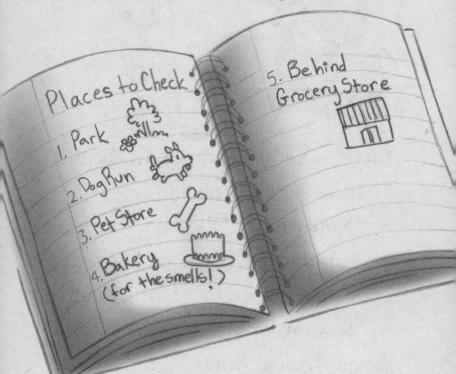

At four thirty Ellie eyed the clock
and jumped up. "I've got to go," she

said. "Nana Gloria is making dinner, and I promised her I'd help."

The girls made plans to meet up the next day. "I'll be at the clinic all morning," Amy said, "but after lunch, we should check these places."

Ellie nodded. "That sounds much better than hanging out with crazy Lenny all day!"

chapter 7

Follow That Puppy!

The next day Amy rode her bike to Ellie's house. Together she and Ellie pedaled toward the park. It was the first place on their list.

"Can you believe today is Wednesday?" Ellie called to Amy. "Spring break is already halfway over!"

Ellie was right! *Wow!* thought

Amy. She had imagined spending the entire week *reading* a mystery. *Time sure does fly when you're solving one!*

On their way to the park, Amy and Ellie passed Liz's house. Amy was shocked to see Liz's family's van in the driveway. "Look!" Amy called. "Liz is back early!"

As the girls parked their bikes, Liz came out of the house. "Yay! Liz!" Ellie cried.

The three girls hugged. "You're back early!" Amy said.

Liz nodded. "We had to cut our beach trip short thanks to Stewart's sunburn. So long, sun and sand . . . and all because *he* forgot to put on sunscreen!"

Stewart was coming around the side of the house. "I heard that!" he said. Stewart's face, arms, and legs were bright red like a tomato.

"Hi, Stewart!" Ellie shouted cheerfully. She gave him a funny little wave.

Stewart was too grumpy to notice. "This day gets worse and worse," he said. "Three hours in the car, sitting on sunburned legs, and now I get pawed by some stray puppy! Man, that really hurt!"

Stewart turned. There, on his shorts, were two muddy paw prints! Amy and Ellie stared. Rufus prints!

They crowded around Stewart. "What puppy?" Amy asked.

"Where?" Ellie cried. "Which way did he go?"

Stewart looked confused. "A Saint Bernard, I think,"

he said. He pointed toward the backyard. "He ran that way."

Amy and Ellie dashed around the side of Liz's house. Liz followed. "Wait up!" she shouted. "What's going on?"

Amy didn't have time to explain.

She and Ellie got to the backyard—just in time to spot Rufus!

Right before he disappeared under the fence.

Amy and Ellie dashed over. "RUFUS!" they shouted. The girls peeked through the fence to watch Rufus run through the neighbor's yard. In seconds, he was gone.

Liz caught up. She looked over the fence too. "Who was that?" she asked.

"Come on," said Amy. "We'll fill you in."

The three girls hurried to the clinic. Amy wanted to tell her mom they'd seen Rufus! On the way, Amy and Ellie told Liz about

Ms. Sullivan's missing puppy.

"Hi, girls!" said Dr. Purvis when she saw them. She was out back by the supply shed. "Hey, Amy, have you seen that new case of Fitter Critter treats?"

Amy remembered it had been delivered the other day. "I put it here by the shed door."

"Huh," Amy's mom said, looking around. "Maybe Gail moved it." She looked at Amy. "So, what's up?"

The girls told her about seeing Rufus in Liz's backyard. Dr. Purvis was excited! "That means Rufus is still in the area and he's okay!" she said. "That's great news!"

Dr. Purvis suggested they put up MISSING PUPPY flyers around town. "I believe one of you loves to draw . . . ?"

Ellie and Amy looked at Liz. She grinned.

The girls worked together. Amy described what Rufus looked like while Liz did the drawing. Amy decided what the flyer should say. Ellie picked an eye-catching shade of hot pink paper for

the flyers. They finished just as
Dr. Purvis was locking up the clinic
for the day.

"Are you guys busy tomorrow?" Amy asked her friends. She would need help putting up the flyers.

Ellie and Liz smiled. "We are now!" Liz said.

chapter 8

A New Lead

Dr. Purvis made copies of the flyer on the clinic's photocopier. Then Amy, Ellie, and Liz spent all day Thursday handing them out. They started with number one on their list of places to check—the park.

Ellie taped a flyer to the notice board by the playground. Meanwhile, Amy checked the field.

Liz looked over by the water fountain for pets. There was no sign of Rufus anywhere.

Next on the list was the dog run.

The girls handed a few flyers to dog owners. No one had seen Rufus, but everyone said they'd look out for him.

The girls headed over to the pet store on Main Street. "I walk by here with Sam sometimes," Ellie said. Sam was her family's golden retriever. "He always stops and barks like crazy."

Amy wasn't surprised. There were always cats in the front window. Today there were some beautiful tabby cats and three cute black-and-white kittens.

Amy froze. There was also something else: a muddy paw print, right on the window glass! "Aha!" she said, pointing.

The girls spoke to the pet store owner. They gave her a flyer. She remembered a dog that looked like Rufus. "Yesterday afternoon. I saw him out front, all alone. When I went to check on him, he ran off. I haven't seen him since."

Amy wrote down the info in her notebook. The girls thanked the

owner and headed for number four on their list, the bakery.

The smell of baking bread and cakes made Amy's mouth water. She'd bet a hungry dog could smell this place from miles away, but no

one at the bakery had seen Rufus.

They hung up more flyers: at the grocery store, the post office, the café, and on every bulletin board downtown.

But they didn't find another clue, until . . .

"What's that?" Ellie asked. Amy had stopped on the town square. She was bending over a piece of trash on the grass.

"Good for you, Amy," said Liz. "We should all do

our part to keep the Earth clean."
Liz and her family were really into
the environment. "Want me to toss
that?"

"No, wait. Know what this is?"
Amy said. She held up the piece of
trash. It was an empty bag of Fitter
Critter treats. "And look here." Amy

pointed to one corner. "It's chewed open."

Ellie and Liz understood and nodded. "By a hungry puppy?" Ellie said.

Amy wrote down the clue in her notebook. The list now took up two pages. There had to be *something* the clues could tell them?

"So, here's what we know," Amy said. She sat down under a shady tree. Ellie and Liz sat down

next to her. "Rufus is leaving paw prints everywhere."

"He's been to the pet store," Ellie added, "and Liz's yard . . . and in front of the clinic . . ."

"His prints are always muddy," said Liz, "even though it hasn't rained since Monday."

"Right!" said Amy. "Hmm. Someplace that's always wet . . . ?" She held up the empty treat bag. "And where did Rufus find these?"

The clues and the events of the last week swirled in Amy's mind.

Then it hit her! Lightbulbs went

off in her head. That case of Fitter Critter treats her mom was looking for . . . The flower bed at the clinic, watered every morning . . . The rustling sound she'd heard from her backyard Monday night . . .

"Of course!" Amy shouted. "I think I know where to find Rufus!" She jumped up and led the girls toward the clinic.

Amy had a plan.

chapter 9

Gotcha!

On Friday morning Amy slowly and quietly ate her cereal. Her mom sipped her coffee. She looked across the table at Amy. "Nothing yet?" she asked.

"Nope," Amy said, shaking her head. "Not yet—"

Clatter, clatter, CRASH! came a noise from outside. Amy's eyes brightened. She jumped up from the table.

Dr. Purvis rushed to look out the back window. "It's Rufus!" she cried. She grabbed the leash they had ready. Together, they darted out the back door.

Rufus was by the metal trash can, which had been knocked over. The lid was off, and a very muddy Rufus was slurping Fitter Critter treats off the driveway. Quickly, Dr. Purvis clipped the leash to his collar.

"Hooray!" Dr. Purvis cheered.

"Amy, I'm so proud of yo
plan really worked!"

Amy grinned. She felt proud of
her plan too. The clues had got her

to thinking. Had Rufus been hanging around the clinic the whole
time? On Thursday afternoon Amy
and her friends had searched all
around the clinic. They didn't find

Rufus, but they did find what was left of the missing case of Fitter Critter treats. They also found lots and lots of Rufus prints.

The girls put a plan in motion. They took a package of Fitter Critters and left a trail of treats leading to Amy's trash can. They put a bunch of treats on the lid so when Rufus jumped up to get them . . . *CRASH!*

"It worked perfectly!" Amy cried.

"Ms. Sullivan will be so happy!" her mom said. "I'll go call her. And then . . ." She looked down at Rufus and pinched her nose.

Amy smelled it too. "Woof . . . Rufus needs a bath!"

chapter 10

Ms. Sullivan's Idea

Amy called Liz and Ellie from the clinic. Liz came over right away. Ellie arrived next. "Look who I found on the way," she said. Marion came in behind her. She held up her blue ribbon. She and Coco had won first place at the horse show! Amy, Liz, and Ellie crowded around her for a group hug.

Rufus ran in from the other room. He put two muddy front paws on Marion's knees. Marion patted him on the head. "Hiya, Rufus," she said. "Ellie was just telling me all about you . . . *and* your muddy paws!"

Rufus wagged his tail. And it didn't stop wagging as the girls splashed, soaped, rinsed, dried, and brushed him.

When they were done, Rufus was one clean and happy dog.

"Wait!" said Marion. "He needs a little something extra." She tied her blue ribbon to Rufus's collar. "Perfect!"

"Awwww," said Amy. "Nice touch, Marion."

"I agree," said Dr. Purvis from the hallway. "Girls, Ms. Sullivan is in the waiting room. How about we bring her this handsome pup?"

Amy noticed her friends looked a little nervous. "Don't worry, guys," she said. "You'll like Ms. Sullivan."

Rufus led the way. He ran right to Ms. Sullivan. She knelt down with her arms wide open. Rufus jumped up and licked her face over and over. She hugged him tight and smiled from ear to ear. "My Rufus!" she cried. "Oh, thank you, Dr. Purvis, and thank you, girls! Amy, your mom told me how you tracked Rufus down. I can't even tell you how grateful I am."

Amy could feel herself blushing, but she didn't mind. "Glad to help, Ms. Sullivan," Amy said quietly.

Ms. Sullivan stood up. "I want to ask you and your friends for help with something else. I was just discussing it with your mom." Dr. Purvis nodded.

"After this Rufus adventure, I've decided that I want to open an animal shelter here in Santa Vista," Ms. Sullivan went on. "I have a big barn that's empty and isn't being used. I thought it might be the perfect spot."

Amy gasped. "What a great idea!" she cried.

Ms. Sullivan smiled. "I'm so glad you think so, Amy. I can't do it alone. I mean, I do have the money and the barn. Dr. Purvis has kindly offered to be the veterinarian for the shelter, but there will be lots of other work to do. Feeding and taking care of the animals . . ." Ms. Sullivan looked at all the girls. "Would you four mind helping me get it started?"

The girls looked at one another, wide-eyed. *"Mind?"* cried Marion.

"Are you serious?" asked Liz.

"It's the most exciting thing that's ever happened to me!" cried Ellie.

Amy jumped up and down. "We'd love to!"

Dr. Purvis smiled at the girls. "Ms. Sullivan, I think you have a deal."

The End and the Beginning

That night the girls were all sitting around Liz's bedroom. It was Friday night and there was time for one more sleepover before spring break was over.

"What a week!" said Liz, drawing in her sketch pad. "That was the shortest beach vacation I've ever had. Thanks to Stewart."

Ellie was pecking out a tune on Liz's electronic keyboard. "Yeah, spring break was not long enough. At least Lenny's singing is getting better," she said, rolling her eyes.

Marion had brought her scrapbook. She was adding photos from

the horse show. "I had a blast at the show," she said, "but I feel like I missed all the fun here!"

It was a fun week in Santa Vista, Amy thought. She'd been so busy that she hadn't had time to finish her Nancy Drew book! Amy looked down at the last page.

> At last, all the clues added up. Nancy could prove that Sandy Jessup had taken the pony. But if Sandy wouldn't admit it, how would Nancy ever find the pony?
>
> Just then, there was a knock at Alice's door. Nancy stood by Alice's side as she opened it. Standing on Alice's front porch was Mr. Gilbert—with the pony!
>
> "I believe this little lady belongs to you?" Mr. Gilbert said. His tone was as gruff as ever, but Nancy could swear she saw a twinkle in his eye.

"That reminds me," said Amy. "Isn't Ms. Sullivan the best?"

The girls all agreed. "You were right, Amy," said Ellie. "We were judging the book by its cover."

"She's not at all what I thought," said Marion. "Can you believe she let us pick the name for the shelter?"

Liz turned her sketch pad around. "Look!" she said. "I drew

up an ad. Maybe we could get it in next week's edition of the *Santa Vista Star*?"

"The Critter Club!" Marion read Liz's poster. "I love the name we came up with," she said happily.

Everyone else nodded.

"I bet Rufus will like the name too!" said Ellie. "It sounds a lot like Fitter Critters, his favorite treat!"

Amy laughed. "As long as we stock the barn with those treats, Rufus won't care *what* we call it!"

She smiled, thinking about all

the other animals that The Critter Club would help. Spring break was almost over, but it felt like the beginning of a big, new adventure.